CONTENTS

FARTY MARTY

A Heartwarming
Tale of Farts
and Friendship

JUSTIN JOHNSON

FARTY MARTY

A HEARTWARMING TALE OF FARTS AND FRIENDSHIP

NIGHT HAD SETTLED IN ON THE FARM. THE stars in the sky were twinkling and the sound of crickets and bull frogs could be heard for miles. The air was clean and crisp. That is, clean and crisp outside the barn.

Inside the barn, where the animals were just nestling into their hay piles for a well earned night of sleep, the air was different. Very, very different.

"Man!" said a sheep named Franklin from the east side of the barn. "What's that funky smell?"

The other animals perked up their heads and tried to identify exactly what that 'funky' smell was. Winnie, a pig, said that it could've been the smell of emissions from a gas guzzling SUV. Dorry, a goat, argued that it wasn't an SUV, but rather a tractor.

"You know how that thing backfires when Farmer Dave turns it off. Stinks to high heaven, don't it?" She looked around the barn for some support from the others. When she didn't get any, she walked out of the barn muttering under her breath.

Franklin stuck his sniffer in the air and took a great big grab of it, both nostrils stretched to capacity. He leaned his head back and started chewing with nothing in his mouth.

He kept sniffing and chewing and eventually worked his way over to a stall in the middle of the barn. It belonged to a cow named Marty.

Marty was not a large cow. He was not a small cow, either. He was a medium cow. But his farts - they were tremendous. They were not the farts of your typical, run-of-the-mill, mid-range cow. They were the farts of a gigantic cow. They had the power to clear a barn full of filthy farm animals. And Marty's butt was in full force tonight.

"I hope you're happy with yourself," Franklin said, looking down at Marty, trying not to choke as he spoke.

Marty put his head down in shame. This wasn't the first time something like this had happened. And it was beginning to happen more and more. At first, it would happen once, maybe twice a month. But lately, it'd been once or twice a week. And this was the second night in a row.

Franklin started to walk back toward the other animals when Marty let loose again. The first fart had been an SBD (Silent But Deadly) that had floated and lingered in the air before enveloping the other farm animals in a festering cloud of funk. The second fart, however, was loud and unproud. It was thrust past Marty's tail with such force that his tail ended up at rest on his back.

Marty looked up to see what Franklin's reaction would be. All Franklin could do was shake his head and walk away.

Marty put his head back down and began to cry. He had to get this under control, but how?

THE SUN CAME UP AND THE ROOSTER CROWED. IT had not been a good night. It had been a night of broken sleep and broken wind.

The animals were slow to get going, casting nasty glances in the direction of Marty's stall. Marty was laying low. Unfortunately, his farts weren't. He didn't think it was possible, but they actually sounded and smelled like they were getting worse. They were louder and smellier than before.

Finally, he stood up and walked past the others and out of the barn. Every step he took produced gas. The other animals turned away and covered their snouts, beaks and bills. One of the animals quipped, "Hey Marty, you just gave Jim Bob freckles!" The other animals fell over in laughter. Marty just put his head down and continued farting his way out of the barn.

He stepped out into the grazing field and the big ball of gas in the sky forced a big ball of gas from Marty's backside. Marty was feeling as low as he could. Earlier the night before, the gas attack had brought him some relief. He'd been feeling some rumblings in his tummy and forcing some air out of his derriere had calmed the storm down a bit...at first.

But as the night dragged on and his belly kept right on a goin' and his butt kept right on a blowin' he started to feel annoyed and self conscious. He couldn't get any sleep and he knew he had a busy day of eating grass and standing in a field ahead of him. If he didn't get some sleep he'd be forced to find a spot of under the tree by the side of the road and lie down in the middle of the day. And then the people in the cars would look at him and point and think that he was one of the lazy cows. They might even call him 'beef jerky,' the worst slight for any cow. And for most of the cows sitting under those shade giving trees, they'd be right. They were the riff raff of the farm. But Marty was...

What was Marty? He didn't really know what he was - now. Now that he was starting to have these farting fits every few nights. He just didn't know what it was that was forcing it, so to speak. He continued to walk around the field and fart, stopping every few steps to take a bite of grass and chew it around. He wasn't even really that hungry, but that's what a cow was supposed to do, eat grass. So that's what he was going to do, whether he was hungry or not.

"Hey," he heard a soft voice from behind him. It was Little Bo Peep, the aptly named sheep.

"I wouldn't stand there if I were you," cautioned Marty. "I'm liable to blow you to smithereens with a fart rocket."

"Oh, right," said Bo Peep. She moved around Marty's body and positioned herself directly across from his face. "I wanted to apologize for the others. It can't be easy going through what you're going through, and listening to them mock you relentlessly has got to make it considerably more difficult."

"Yeah," Marty said, his head down and a mouthful of grass going through some mechanical digestion. "It was a hard night. But I'm okay. I just wish I could figure out how to stop it."

"That's actually why I'm here," Bo Peep said. "I've noticed that lately you've been farting more - a lot more. I've also noticed that you've been spending quite a bit of time over near the pig pen."

Marty could feel himself starting to get defensive.

What was Bo Peep getting at? Had she come over here to help him, or make him feel worse? "So? What does that have to do with my farting?"

"Just calm down for a minute," Bo Peep said, noting the aggressive tone in Marty's voice. "Hear me out before you get all upset and jump down my throat."

Marty knew she was right. He did everything he could, short of laying down in the grass, to relax himself. If he wanted things to get better, he needed to listen to her.

At that moment, Farmer Dave was walking by with a friend. He was showing off the farm, which he often did on nice days such as this one. Marty noticed that the man walking with Farmer Dave was scrunching his face up. He asked, "What's that smell Dave? It's horrible!"

Farmer Dave stuck out his thumb and motioned toward Marty. "I think we just got crop dusted." He chuckled a little.

His friend didn't laugh, but rather asked him what 'crop dusting' was.

"Crop dusting's when someone walks by and lets one rip and they just keep right on a walkin'."

The friend nodded and the two continued their walk, leaving Marty feeling more upset than he already was. He put his head down and kept chewing absentmindedly at the grass.

"So, as I was saying," Bo Peep continued, "I think I have a way to help you out."

Marty listened to Bo Peep's plan. He farted through most of it and was thankful that she was in front of him, instead of behind him.

She laid it out perfectly, how he could get his flatulence under control so he would be more comfortable and the other animals wouldn't pick on him.

It was pretty simple, actually. "As I started to say earlier," Bo Peep began, "You've been spending a lot of time down in the pig pen. And you can deny it all you want to - but I've seen you sticking your mug in their trough."

Marty nodded, and if a cow was capable of turning red from embarrassment, he surely would have. Bo Peep noticed his eyes were filled with shame. That was enough to convince her that he was willing to accept that he had done something wrong and move on.

"What I'm suggesting for you, is that you stay in your own field and graze on the grass. That's cow's food - grass. You never know what kind of things are going to be in the pig troff. And quite frankly, it's alright for them - they're not picky. But your diet should be managed a little more carefully."

"You think it's that easy?" Marty asked. He was

willing to give it a try, but somehow he thought that it might involve something a little more…complicated.

"Watch out Bo Peep!" The shout came from the over-protective sheep, Franklin, who was just emerging from the fart filled barn and into the fart filled pasture. "I hope his breath smells better than his butt."

A couple of the other animals could be heard laughing inside the barn. Marty looked at Bo Peep, begging her with his eyes to stick up for him. But she didn't. "If you want this to stop, Marty, you're going to have to do it yourself."

"Can you help me stay away from the pig pen?" he asked. "I don't know if I have the will power to do it alone."

Bo Peep nodded. "That, I can help you with. But dealing with the other animals is going to be up to you."

Marty thanked Bo Peep and then headed over to a lonely tree and stood by himself to think things through. He could do this. He knew that Bo Peep would help him out and once he got everything back to normal, his issues with the other animals would end. And then he pushed out a massive fart, that ended up turning into a massive poop, filled with lots of previously yummy pig troughey goodness.

All things pass in time, he thought to himself.

IT WAS DAY TWO OF THE GRASS ONLY DIET AND Marty was feeling cranky. He was still sure that this is what he wanted to do, but he was finding himself getting the shakes, the sweats and the poo poos associated with such a drastic change in routine.

"I just can't win," he complained to Bo Peep. "When I eat what's bad for me, I fart uncontrollably and everybody hates me. When I eat what's good for me, I poop uncontrollably and hate myself."

"It's okay," Bo Peep encouraged, "Just hang in there and stick with it. It'll get easier and you'll begin to feel better in a few more days."

Marty nodded and walked away, doubting that this would be the case. But he had told Bo Peep that he would give her way a try, at least for a while.

The rest of the morning went by and he found himself up by the side of the road with the other cows. He pulled up a spot under the tree next to one of them.

"What's your name?" the cow asked.

"Marty," Marty answered shortly.

"I don't think I've ever seen you before." The cow leaned over and grabbed a mouthful of grass with a dandelion. Marty noticed how loudly he chewed and wondered if this was simply a result of feeling hungry and sensitive.

"I don't spend a lot of time over on this side of the

farm," Marty said, trying to be as kind as possible. And not wanting to be rude he asked, "What's your name?"

"Jerry," the cow answered. "So, you said you don't spend much time over here. What brings you here today?"

"I'd rather not say." Marty shifted uncomfortably.

"Hey man, whatever it is, you can tell old Jerry."

Marty thought about this for a moment, weighing his options. He didn't know Jerry and it would be rather uncomfortable to share his struggles with a complete stranger. On the other hand, he hadn't run into Jerry after two years on the farm. If he shared what he was going through and things went poorly, the likelihood of Marty seeing Jerry again, especially if he didn't want to, were slim. And if things went really well and Jerry could offer some words of encouragement or help him out a bit, that would be a bonus.

"I've been having this issue," Marty started, thinking *what the hay*. "You see, I don't always like to eat the grass and I sometimes find myself snacking over at the pig trough. They get scraps of all sorts of food that doesn't really get along too well with my stomachs."

"Tell me about it," Jerry said.

"Well, I've been eating over there more and more and - wait a minute!" Marty stopped and stared at Jerry. "Did you just say, 'tell me about it'?"

"Yeah man," Jerry replied. "I got into the trough the

other night while they were asleep. I've had the runs for a good day and a half."

"Right," said Marty, bobbing his head up and down. "So you know exactly what I'm going through. The other animals are giving me a really hard time because...well, you know. I stink."

"Yup, yup. I hear that!"

"My friend Bo Peep has designed a plan for me, where I only eat grass for the rest of my life. So far, I'm having some trouble with it. I'm pooping like crazy, I have the sweats and I can't stop thinking about the deliciousness that I'm missing out on."

"Aw man, no," said Jerry shaking his head. "You see, that's always what everyone's trying to do. They want you to give up on doing the things that you love, just because you have a little bit of gas."

"Are you saying that Bo Peep's not right?"

"Not entirely. She's partially right. We really don't belong near the pig troff. It does do some pretty weird things to our stomachs. But the idea that we can never eat anything besides grass is, perhaps, a bit extreme. In my experience, life's about balance."

Marty raised an eyebrow, looking at Jerry for the first time as something a little more substantial than 'beef jerky'. "What do you mean, balance?"

Jerry looked over his shoulder. "Do you see that cow over there?"

"Yeah." They were looking at a cow Marty'd seen a few times before. Marty was pretty sure he'd never seen him move from that spot.

"That's Don," Jerry said. "He's sat there for the better part of six months. He gets up to eat, poop and pee. That's it. He doesn't walk around and try mingle with the other cows. He refuses to speak to any animal that's not a cow. At first, the other cows made an effort to go over and talk to him. But he's a broken record, only talking about chewing grass and the weather. Eventually, the other cows started to give up on him. Now, he just sits there and has no friends in the world. It's because he's got no balance. He's one note."

Marty tried not to stare at Don. The sun was shining brightly on his back and his face was resting on an overgrown section of field. He looked sad and lonely.

"Sometimes," Jerry continued, "you have to go out and experience something new. Otherwise, you could end up like old Don."

This got Marty to thinking. He thought that for the next few weeks, he would keep to himself and work on the whole grass eating thing. Bo Peep was onto something. And while Jerry thought that it was okay for cows to go 'live a little' over by the pig troff, Marty knew that this early in his change, it would probably do more harm than good. After he got back into the right habits for a cow, he would venture out little by little an find out what he could handle and what might be too much.

"It was nice talking to you Jerry," Marty said, standing up. Jerry gave a nod and continued chewing his grass, staring off into the distance. Marty turned and walked back toward the barn ready to start turning things around.

IT WAS THREE DAYS BEFORE MARTY'S DIARRHEA and wet farts subsided. It was a long three days, but he made it through them. Bo Peep was great. She continued to coach Marty through his ordeal and never stopped encouraging him, even when the other animals told her she was nuts for hanging out with 'Farty Marty'.

Marty had been given a new nickname. He wasn't overly fond of it, but hey, what was he going to do? The way he looked at it, he could either get upset and lash out at them over it - which would no doubt have made things worse, or he could take that insulting name - Farty Marty - and use it to make himself better. It took a lot of self control and discipline on Marty's part. And on occasion it did bother him, especially at first. But cows have a way of developing a thick skin and moving forward.

It was about a week after Marty had stopped eating at

the pig trough. The sun was setting and night was coming up over the barn. All the animals were filing in for the night, their busy days of eating and running around were over. It was time to nestle into a bed of hay and call it a day.

Marty approached Bo Peep. "I just wanted to say thank you for helping me get my life back on track."

"It's nothing, Marty. You'd have figured it out eventually, I just gave you a little nudge in the right direction," she said.

"Well, nonetheless, it means the world to me and I wanted to let you know."

"I appreciate that," she said. "Good night Marty." Bo Peep nestled down into a small pile of hay in the front corner of the barn and prepared to sleep.

Marty turned and headed back to his place near the middle of the barn and tried to get comfy. And then he felt something that gave him a start. It was working its way through his cavernous bowels and right toward his behind. It had been several days since he had a poop, or an overly stinky fart. He laid down in his bedding and closed his eyes, hoping it would pass. A minute went by, then two. Marty was trying to hold it in, knowing what would happen if he let it out as everyone was trying to get to sleep.

Eventually, however, the fart escaped. *Pppfffff.* It sailed out into the wide open barn and Marty closed his eyes, pretending to be asleep, hoping this would cut down on some of the insults. As he breathed, he could smell the air change slightly. It was a matter of a few breaths before he smelt what he had dealt. And then he knew everything would be A-OK. The smell was more sweet than repugnant. And it was gone, within matter of seconds, as if it was blown away by the wind. It did not hang in the air like a wet towel on a clothesline. Rather it drifted off like the white fuzz of a dandelion, wistful and light.

He perked his ears slightly, expecting to hear even just a little bit of an uproar from the front of the barn. But the only thing he heard were snores. Everyone kept right on sleeping and didn't notice that floating gas from Marty's butt one bit.

Marty took a deep breath and nestled himself back into his hay bed.

Ahh, he thought to himself, *Grass farts.*

FLiCK!

A story of a booger searching for his purpose

JUSTIN JOHNSON

FLICK!

A STORY OF A BOOGER SEARCHING FOR HIS PURPOSE

FLICK'S LIFE BEGAN ONE DAY AGO. HE WAS JUST a little speck of dust floating in the air, when Timmy took a deep breath and sucked the dust up his left nostril.

Flick felt himself floating upwards and then noticed the darkness. He tried to turn around and float away, but he became entangled in a gnarly nose hair. The hair was thick and coarse. It said, "Not so fast!" when it got its curly little rings around Flick.

"Let me go!" Flick yelled, trying as hard as a dust particle could to squirm his way out of the nose hair's grasp. "I have so much life to live. I'm too young to be trapped in here, all alone."

The nose hair simply laughed and said, "You're quite

right about having a life to live. However, you are exactly the right age to be trapped in here."

Flick squiggled and wiggled, trying more desperately than before to free himself from the grasp of the tangly strand.

"I already told you, I can't let you go. You must stay here and live out your days with me."

"But why?" Flick wondered.

"That's just the nature of everything. Didn't your parents ever teach you anything?"

"No, I never met my parents. I heard that they were both taken away in very tragic accidents. My father had been floating through the air one day and became stuck to a dog's behind. A skunk sprayed the dog and the dog's owner was forced to give it a long overdue bath. My father was swept away with the bath water." At this thought, Flick began to cry uncontrollably.

The nose hair tightened it's grip a little, not in a menacing or threatening way, but almost like a hug. "There, there little guy. It's okay. You'll be alright. Do you want to talk about what happened to your mother? You know, get it out in the open?"

Flick nodded, to the degree that a dust particle could. "My mother was sitting on a coffee table, watching my father through the window when he had been taken by the dog I just mentioned. She cried out for him and was in the process of trying to become airborne when, sadly, she was struck down by a paper towel full of Pledge. What those fine folks have against dust, I'll never know."

"I'm sorry to hear that little guy," the nose hair empathized.

After he'd finished crying, Flick took a second look around the cave he now found himself in. He noticed that he was not the only dust particle trapped in here. His eyes moved from one particle to the next, each one nuzzled up with a coarse black hair. Some of these were considerably bigger than Flick. And they had begun to change color.

Flick looked at himself. He was almost white, like he'd been plucked from a cotton undershirt. But as he looked around he could see that some of the particles that had grown to double or triple his size were starting to look tan, almost brown. And there was one that looked like the big boss man. He was fat and green.

Flick wanted desperately to speak to him. He looked like he'd been here for a long time and was doing alright.

"Hey," Flick said to his nose hair, "Do you see that big guy up there? What's his story?"

The nose hair replied, "That's Bogie. He's been here longer than anyone else. Come to think of it, he's been here longer than any other dust particle I've ever seen."

"Is he nice?" Flick asked. And then realizing how

strange that question probably sounded, he rephrased, "What I mean is, do you think he would talk to me if I asked him some questions?"

"Oh," The nose hair said, stumped. Nobody had ever asked this question before. "I don't see why he wouldn't answer your question."

Just as the nose hair was finishing up his thought, a rumble could be felt. It came quickly, as three quick jolts, forcing Flick and the others further upward. After the third jolt Flick could see the opening to the cave go dark. Inside the cave there was a strong feeling of tension and anticipation as everyone, in their own way, prepared for the impending storm. They sensed the end was near and wanted to be prepared to handle it with grace and dignity.

Finally, the opening to the cave shone bright with light, and Flick could feel the entire cave tilt upward. He could see the room he'd been in just moments ago. His vantage changed from the floor, to the wall, to the ceiling...and then he didn't see anything.

He had closed his eyes when the storm hit. It felt like hurricane level winds were working their way through the cave, forcing the other particles to hold on for dear life. A few of the particles flew past Flick, the looks of sheer terror on their faces made Flick instinctively tighten his grip on his nose hair. Surprisingly, his nose hair did not reciprocate the grip, but rather attempted to let go of Flick.

When it seemed like everything was over and Flick was still inside the cave, he began to climb his way back up onto his nose hair. As he was just about back to his spot, another jolt shook the cave. And this time, even more of the particles came flying by. Flick, again, managed to hold on, but barely.

Pulling himself back up, he noticed that Bogie was no longer perched high above. During the storm and the aftermath, he'd somehow been forced closer to the opening of the cave.

For the time being, the storm was over and Flick found himself eye to eye with Bogie. He didn't think it was possible, but Bogie looked even a little more intimidating up close than he had when he was several millimeters away.

Flick was torn. He desperately wanted to get some answers from what was clearly the most senior dust particle in the nose. But he also had the decency to understand that everyone had just been through quite a traumatic ordeal and to push Bogie at this time probably wasn't the most compassionate of decisions.

"Are you alright?" he found himself asking. He was very proud of himself for finding a compassionate, yet definite way to get response.

"Yeah, kid, I'm fine," Bogie managed. "Just need a minute to catch my breath."

"Okay," Flick said, "if there's anything I can do for you, just let me know. I'm happy to help."

Bogie tried to stifle his laughter, but couldn't.

"What's so funny?" Flick wondered aloud. "Why are you laughing? I didn't say anything funny."

"It's nothing," Bogie said, trying to compose himself. "I was just thinking about the endless possibilities of ways that you might be able to help before I realized that there's absolutely nothing you can do."

"What do you mean? There's lots I can do!"

"Name something," Bogie challenged between laughs.

Flick tried to think of something he could do to help. Nothing came to mind. He looked at his situation and realized the reality of it. He was being held captive by a hair, who only let go when that giant gust of wind came through the cave. He was much smaller than Bogie, so even if he could get free, anything that Bogie might ask him to do in the way of propping or pushing would be too much for Flick. The only thing Flick could really think of was companionship.

"I can be your friend. That's what I can do. I can be here when you need me, to talk about anything and everything you want to talk about. We can talk about nothing if you want, or we can talk about everything. I'm here with nowhere to go and you're here with nowhere to go. We might as well make the most of it."

Bogie was taken aback. He'd expected Flick, as all of

the other dust particles had done, to give up and ignore him. As the elder of the cave, he was finding it increasingly difficult to find others he could relate to. They were all much too young, with little or no experience doing much of anything. They ignored him. He had begun to feel disconnected from his fellow dust particles. Over the minutes and hours, he had collected an accumulation of dirt and experiences that had taken its toll and left him isolated.

But now, he was here, face to face with a young and sprightly dust particle who wanted more than anything in the world to be friends.

"Friend, you say? Well, that sounds just lovely. We should give that a try."

Flick smiled as much as a dust particle could and said, "I'd like that. How do we start?"

"I think we already have," Bogie replied. "But if you want to make it formal, you could start by telling me your name."

"Flick. My name is Flick. You don't have to tell me your name. I've already been told it's Bogie. I do have a question for you, if I may."

"Of course."

"Well, I've been here for about twenty minutes now," Flick began. "I really have no idea what I'm supposed to do. What do we do here?"

"That's a good question," Bogie replied. "I've found

myself wondering the same thing. And to be perfectly honest with you, I don't know if anyone really knows. I guess, if I had to give an answer I would say that we sit here on our hair and do the best we can until it's time to go."

"What do you mean time to go?"

Bogie was silent for a moment as he thought about the best way to phrase his response. "You know, Flick, I was once where you are now - Sitting on a nose hair, freshly sucked into the cave, afraid of what may lie ahead, wondering what I'm to do with my life. I've seen many dust particles come and go. Some of them had been old and crusty when it was their time and others were like you, young and spry. They all at one point asked what they were supposed to do. And to be honest with you, I don't know if I'm really the best one to answer that question for you."

This answer came as both a surprise and a disappointment to Flick. He figured who would be better to ask this question to than the dust particle with the most life experience. When he didn't get an answer it left him with even more questions then he had before.

"If you're not the best one to answer that question, who is?"

"Well," Bogie began, "in my experience, I've found that it's not really up to other dust particles to tell you what you make of yourself. I can tell you what I've done, but ultimately you'll have to make up your own mind and do what you believe is right."

"Alright," Flick said, "can you tell me what you've done then, so I have something to think about?"

"When I got here, I was a lot like you. After spending most of my life to that point just floating around looking for my next place to land, I'd been sucked up here. There was no hope of escape and so I had a lot of time to sit and think. After a while, I found myself attracting different types of things, mostly dirt and muck. It collected on me and held me down. I went through a number of different feelings, mostly despair and hopelessness. Occasionally anger would creep in. And then I started asking questions to anyone who would listen. I asked what was happening to me; I asked why I had to stay here; I asked what my purpose was. After receiving no answer for quite a lengthy period of time, I asked the nose hair that held me so tightly, 'Why do you hold me so tightly? Why can't you just let me go and be free?' And he responded by saying it was his job. He had to grab any dust that might make it inside the boy's body. When I asked why, he told me that if I were to get past him, I could make the boy very ill. He said that while he felt bad for me, it was his duty to protect the boy."

Bogie fell silent. Flick began thinking about all that

Bogie had said. Was he really going to be here forever? Was he going to become angry and despair in the way Bogie had? Or would knowing how Bogie's life had turned out help him understand his own?

"After all this time," Flick pressed, "what would you say *your* purpose is?"

Bogie didn't answer right away. He gave the question time to marinate in his mind. "I guess I would say that my purpose has been to protect this boy, just like the nose hairs. I'm not quite as active as they are. I'm not able to reach out and grab things the way they can. But I certainly have stopped enough dirt and grime from making its way into the boy's body. And eventually, it will be my time to go. I will be thrust out the same way I came in, not really sure what my fate might be."

Flick thought on that for a moment. The idea that he was helping the boy was a good feeling. He wondered if he was meant to accrue as much dirt as Bogie or if his path would be different. He wondered how many dust particles Bogie had seen come and go.

As he was having this thought, a darkness came over the cave and Flick looked downward toward the opening. Something was coming toward him, closing the cave off from all light. In the darkness, Flick could hear a loud scraping sound, followed by a few groans and a few screams. When the light flooded the cave's entrance again, he noticed that several of the dust particles that had been lining the edges of the cave were gone.

These particles were larger than Flick, but not nearly as big as Bogie.

"Guess it was their time," Bogie said. "A shame really, they were doing such a good job keeping the dirt up near the front of the cave."

Flick looked out beyond where these particles had been and noticed that they were on the end of a large rounded surface. There were deep ridges formed on top, and along the side was a sharp, shiny surface. The formation started to move back in the direction of the cave and then was suddenly thrust beneath the cave's opening. Flick could feel an up and down motion and he could hear a sloshing sound.

Flick asked Bogie, "What just happened?"

"I've seen it a few times before," Bogie said. "Every time, that thing's entered the cave and taken a few of us away I've heard a voice from outside the cave tell the boy, 'stop eating your boogers'. But to be honest with you, I'm not quite sure what any of that means."

After a moment, Bogie spoke again. "Can I tell you something, Flick?"

"Of course," Flick answered.

"When the darkness overtakes us like that, I become extremely fearful. I worry that it's going to be my turn to be taken away and eaten like a 'booger'. I do not wish to be taken. But I know that I have been here longer than any of the others. It's just a matter of time."

This thought made Flick sad. But he didn't have long to think because just as he was getting ready to tell Bogie the he hoped they wouldn't be taken for a long time, a strong wind began from the top of the cave. This wind was different from the wind that had blown Flick around earlier, and it was different from the wind that had send Bogie to a different hair. This wind was steady and intentional.

It was a constant force against Flick. He feared that he would not be able to hang on as he had done before. He saw a white sheet at the mouth of the cave. It had emerged, seemingly out of nowhere. He felt his grip slipping and looked toward Bogie, whose grip was also in jeopardy of letting go. Flick looked toward the top of the cave and saw other dust particles of various sizes flying right at him, shooting through the air at a rapid rate. He heard their thuds as they were catapulted into the white sheet.

And then everything calmed down. Flick began to climb back up. He looked to Bogie to see how he was doing. But Bogie wasn't there. He looked down toward the mouth of the cave and saw Bogie lying on the white sheet on the outside of the cave. Flick tried to yell, but couldn't find his voice. And then, before he could fully grasp what was happening, the white sheet was folded over Bogie. Bogie was gone in an instant. The sight of fresh white cloth blocking Flick's view sent a panic through him.

Then the wind started up again and took Flick with it. Before he knew what had happened, he was lying on the white sheet and it was being crumpled up around him. He could feel himself being jostled back and forth and up and down. And then he felt something within him rise as he began to plummet. Feeling sick and fearing the unknown of what might happen when he finally landed, he closed his eyes and said just one word: "Please."

The tumult stopped in a matter of a second. The landing was soft. Flick couldn't see anything. He felt alone, as he had upon entering the cave. "Is there anybody here?" he asked after a moment. He waited.

And then it came. The familiar voice of Bogie. "We're here kid. Don't worry about a thing. You're going to be okay."

"Bogie? I'm so glad to hear your voice!" Flick said. "But I can't see you."

"I can't see you either. Can't see anyone as a matter of fact."

"Well this is terrible." Flick could feel the tears coming up now, no matter how hard he tried to keep them down. "What do we do now?"

The answer didn't come at first. Bogie took his time

thinking about things. Flick waited patiently. Finally, Bogie said, "We adjust."

And that's just what Bogie and Flick did. They learned how to live wrapped up in a tissue at the bottom of a trash bag. Though they couldn't see each other, they had a great many wonderful conversations about anything and everything any of us could imagine. And they were happy.

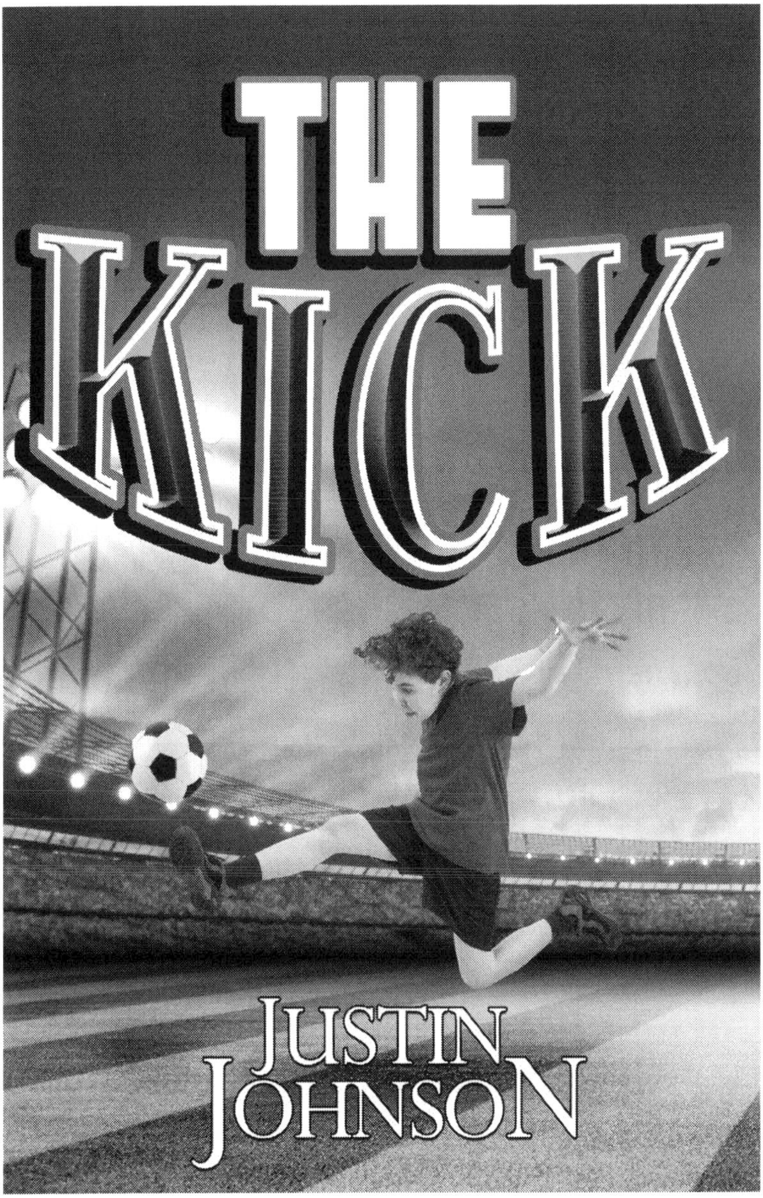
THE
KICK
JUSTIN
JOHNSON

THE KICK

Tommy sat on the bench staring down at the grass. A tiny black bug was climbing one of the longer blades. Tommy kicked at it with his mud caked shoe and watched as it flew away.

"That was mean," said the girl sitting next to him. Her name was Skyy and she'd sat next to Tommy on this bench every Saturday for the past two months. It was soccer season and her mother had signed her up, thinking it would somehow be good for her to get out there and try something new. The same had been true for Tommy, except it was his father who'd been the one to sign him up.

Neither one of them liked it very much. Not because they weren't any good at it, although that didn't help. No, they didn't like it because it wasn't their thing. It wasn't what they were interested in and they had been pushed to do it by people who thought they should.

Skyy was into drawing. She had an easel in her bedroom and what was probably the largest collection of markers and water color paints in the state. If she would've been aloud to, she'd have sat in her room for hours on end, staring out the window and looking down to the brook below. It was beautiful and the brook cut her backyard almost perfectly in half. There was so much to watch. The fish would swim, the bees would zip from one flower to another, and the butterflies would flutter along as though they had not a care in the world. She would take these images and roll them around in her mind and then pick up a brush, or a marker. Hours later she would have another glorious creation - and this made her happy.

Tommy, on the other hand, was into books. He couldn't draw, and he wasn't very good at sports. But he was a thinker. He loved to read and think about how he would do the things the characters did in the story. He would ask himself questions as he read to challenge his own points of view. He'd been reading a lot of sports books lately, trying to figure out why people liked to play them so much. So far, he hadn't been able to figure it out.

And then something happened that would change his life forever!

"How bad is it?" Coach Zimmer asked. He was a tall man with a slender build. He was one of those guys that could run for hours without getting winded. He was reacting to two of the team's best players running into one another. It looked as if the two had banged their knees together. "Are they going to be able to play anymore?"

The head trainer, Bob, trotted over and said, "It looks like they'll be fine, but they both need a few minutes. Do you have anyone you can put in?"

Coach Zimmer looked toward his bench at the two players sitting there. He brought his hand up to his head and rubbed it along the side of his hair. It looked like he was in agony. And given the fact that his choices were Skyy and Tommy, he probably was.

"Skyy, Tommy," he called. They looked up and he motioned them over. Confused, they looked at each other and shrugged their shoulders. They ran over to their coach. "You're going to go in for Wilson and Brody. They need a few minutes to shrug things off."

Tommy felt his stomach tighten and the breath seemed to leave his lungs quicker than usual. He didn't have asthma, but he felt like he did. He was starting to lose the feeling in his fingers. Skyy, on the other hand, was not nervous at all. In fact, she was put off. "Do I have to?" she asked.

"I would really appreciate it," Coach Zimmer said.

"Oh, alright," she sighed, unzipping her warm up jacket and handing it to him.

They both trotted out onto the field to play their first *real* soccer of the year.

THE GAME WAS TIED. THIS WAS DEFINITELY NOT a scenario either one of them had dreamt up the night before as they laid their heads down on their pillows before drifting off to dream land. Neither one of them had played a minute all year, and now here they were in a tie game. What was more, the team was undefeated and if they won today they'd end the season with the best record in the league.

Skyy walked out onto the grass and took her spot near the sideline. She wanted to stay as far from wherever the ball was as she could. Coach Zimmer gave her a thumbs up, believing that Skyy keeping out of the way was probably the best course of action.

Tommy sprinted out toward his place on the field - left wing. Offense. He was jumping up and down, shaking his arms and legs, bobbing his head back and forth, trying to loosen every muscle in his body. He was nervous, but now all of the sudden he felt an emotion he had not expected to feel - excitement. All of his reading over the past several weeks, trying to understand how people could possibly like this game, was starting to come into focus. He found himself overtaken by a sudden surge of adrenaline...and the ball wasn't even back in play yet.

After a minute, the referee finished his conversation with Coach Zimmer and handed the ball to Rusty Tolbert to toss the ball in. He did, and it was promptly taken and dribbled by Steven Zimmer, the coach's son. He had great ball handling skills. He was so smooth and languid, the way he gently tapped the ball from one instep to the other. A defender approached and he calmly planted his left foot in front of the ball and tapped it behind his left leg, changing direction in an instant and making the defender look foolish.

Tommy was running right along side him, about fifteen feet away on the wing. He was all alone. Nobody was guarding him at all! There were five players defending Steven and the right wing, Derek Winslow. They didn't pass him the ball, didn't even look his way and after a few attempts to play a two man game, the ball was stolen by the other team and brought to the other end of the field.

The team's goalie Michelle Blankins, lived up to her name and stopped an attempt on goal before punting the ball to group of mid-fielders. The ball almost hit Skyy on the way down, but Rusty Tolbert rushed over from the center of the field and took the ball on the second hop and passed it effortlessly to Steven Zimmer.

Steven and Derek attempted another round of keep the ball away from Tommy. Again, the result was the same, with one exception. Michelle did not stop the shot.

The team was now down 2-1 heading into the last five minutes of the game.

Coach Zimmer called a timeout and all the players joined him on the sideline. Once everyone was huddled around, he dropped to one knee and looked up at the group of players gathered around. "I'm afraid I have some bad news."

COACH ZIMMER COULD FEEL THE GAZE OF THE team on him, like the sun on the hottest day of summer. Tommy could feel his mouth dry up and he swallowed hard.

"Wilson and Brody are done for today. Their injuries are nothing too serious, but I've discussed things with the medical staff and their parents and we all agree that they should sit and nurse their injuries rather than subject themselves to further harm."

A collective groan could be heard by the team. Coach Zimmer continued. "We are down by one. Our offense has been non-existent since Brody went out, and our defense has been porous. We're leaving Michelle way too open for their players. They are attacking harder than we are. Steven," he said, addressing his son, "You need to give Tommy a chance to handle the ball. The two man game with Derek isn't working. Give him a chance and see what he can do."

Steven started to argue, but Coach Zimmer shot him a look and put his finger up in the air, letting Steven know that he'd better keep it closed and do what he was told. And then he looked at Skyy.

"Skyy, I am going to move you to left defender." Skyy was taken aback by this. She looked at him quizzically. "I know what you're thinking. But, listen, I've seen you in practice. You're tenacious when you want to be. You can really get after it. You don't have a lot of skill, but what you do have is a wild heart. Now's the time you're going to put that to use on the soccer field."

Skyy nodded. Coach Zimmer was right, and everybody knew it. Skyy did have an aggressive streak. And the time for careful play was over. They were down by one, with five minutes left and a perfect season on the line. It was time to throw caution to the wind and play like there was no tomorrow.

The team broke the huddle and headed back out onto the field, ready to pull out a victory.

THE BALL WAS BACK IN PLAY AND STEVEN WAS

dribbling it down the field, his father's words etched in his brain. The defenders were all shifted to the right side of the formation, expecting the pass to go to Derek. Steven, played into this, heading right and then he passed the ball left to Tommy.

Tommy knew that Coach Zimmer had told Steven to do this, but was somehow still caught off guard when he saw the ball rolling in his direction. He looked down at it, not wanting to let it by him. He closed both legs and allowed the ball to bump his shin guards and roll to a stop in front of him. And then he looked up.

The defenders who'd been over on Derek's side of the field were now rushing toward him. *Stay Calm*, he told himself, *Don't Panic*. Easier said than done.

When the defenders were almost upon him, Tommy noticed Steven sprinting toward the goal. Tommy made a kick at the ball. It wasn't a perfect kick, not even close. He grazed the top of the ball, rather than hitting it flush in the middle. But it was enough to get the ball to Steven while the defenders were still rushing at Tommy.

Before they could change direction, Steven had taken a shot and sailed the ball into the top right corner of the goal, just past the outstretched arms of the goalie.

The crowd cheered! They had tied the game and part of it was because of Tommy's pass! Tommy felt a rush like he'd never felt before and now he understood why people liked this game.

Skyy was still down at the far end of the field. She wasn't quite feeling the same way as Tommy. She was still very bored. And to top it all off, she was starting to get cold.

All that was about to change.

The other team put the ball into play and headed toward Skyy and Michelle. They purposely played to Skyy's side of the field, knowing she was inexperienced. What they didn't know was that behind that artistic and disinterested exterior, was a girl who more than anything else hated to be embarrassed.

As the boy came at her with the ball, juking right then left, Skyy charged him, putting on a press he hadn't been expecting. He panicked, and rather than pass the ball to a teammate, he let loose on the ball, kicking it well over the top of the goal.

Skyy could hear her coach and some people from the stands calling out, "good job," and, "way to go!" She could hear it, but it was like her mind was outside of her body. It felt surreal and imagined. Could this really be happening? Could people actually be cheering for her?

When Michelle kicked the ball back into play, there was less than two minutes left in the game. A mid-fielder named Tyler took the ball past midfield and Coach Zimmer called timeout.

Everyone gathered around and the coach had a very short message for the team.

"You've come this far gang. This is your chance. It's a tie game. This is probably the last shot you're going to have at scoring and finishing the season undefeated. Just do what you do best, and things will fall into place. All in!"

Everyone put their hand in the middle of the huddle. "Team on three," Coach said.

"One, two three," and then everyone in unison shouted, "Team!"

Steven took the inbound pass and dribbled as he had the last time. The defenders again played to the right and left Tommy all alone. They must've thought the last time was a fluke. Honestly, so did Tommy.

Nonetheless, he stood there, poised for whatever might come his way. This time, however, Steven did not pass to Tommy. He went to the right as he had every other time and then quickly changed direction and headed toward his left. That got the defense to shift and Tommy was wondering if he'd be able to handle the ball with the defenders that close to him.

A call came in from Coach Zimmer. "Twenty Seconds!"

Steven had to move quickly. Just as it looked as though he was going to pass the ball to Tommy, he made another move and cut straight toward the goal. He kicked the ball as hard as he could on a rope. The goalie reached out and got his hands on it. It looked like the game would end in a tie.

However, the ball was traveling so fast that the goalie couldn't catch it. It bounced off his hands and started bouncing toward Tommy. The defenders were frantically running toward the ball, trying to kick it out of the area. Tommy came in and managed to get just enough of a foot on it to send it traveling past the goalie's left side and into the net.

"Goal!" Steven yelled.

And then the referee blew the whistle. The game was over. Tommy had scored the winning goal! And the team capped off an undefeated season!

Steven and Derek picked Tommy up and put him on their shoulders. At the other end of the field Michelle and Tyler picked Skyy up and put her on their shoulders.

The were finally put down as they reached the sideline.

The team celebrated and each player took turns giving Skyy and Tommy high fives and pats on the back. Skyy's mother and Tommy's father joined the other parents in congratulating the team on their tremendous victory.

After the excitement had died down a little, Michelle approached Skyy. "A few of us get together on the weekends when soccer season ends. We play little pick up games in the park downtown. If you want to join us sometime, we'll leave a spot open for you."

Skyy looked up at her mother, "Can I mom?"

"Of course, honey," her mother said, with a smile and a wink.

On the way to the car, Tommy asked, "Hey dad, do you think I could get a soccer ball?"

"What for?"

"So I can practice."

"What are you going to practice for? I thought you hated soccer. Didn't you tell me you weren't going play next year?" his father asked.

Tommy looked up at his dad with a sly grin, sweat dripping down his face. "Let's just say, I'm reconsidering."

The Dance Recital

Justin Johnson

THE DANCE RECITAL

I'M STARING AT THE CEILING WAITING FOR MY alarm clock to go off. This will be followed by mother barging into my room and telling me it's time to get ready for school. Then the day will officially begin. However, my day began about two hours ago.

I was in the middle of a dream. There was a stage. There was an auditorium full of people. There were bright lights all coming together to form a giant pool of light in the center of the stage. It was dead quiet - and then someone coughed. And I felt a nudge in my back and realized they were all waiting for me.

That's when I woke up.

My name's Gina Wilson. I'm ten years old and today is the day of my big dance recital. The problem is, I'm nervous beyond nervous. I woke up from my little dream

I was just telling you about sweating and crying and the whole shebang. I'm not really sure what shebang means, but I hear my mother use it all the time and she always sounds excited by it. So, I'm guessing it would fit here.

Anyhow, it's almost 6:30. Time for me to get out of bed and begin thinking about how I'm going to tackle school for the day. I really don't know how I'm going to do it. All I can think of is that dance recital, but that's not happening until 6:30 tonight.

Oh boy, oh boy, I'm so knotted up inside. I can't think about anything else. The real problem is, they aren't all good thoughts. Mostly, I'm thinking about what'll happen when I fall down in front of everybody. Will they give me time to get up and dust myself off and try again, like my dance teacher does during practice? Or will they let out one of those large gasps, like what I've done is the worst thing ever? Or even worse, will they laugh at me?

These are the thoughts that are racing through my mind as I head to school for the day. The last one is on my mind the most. It keeps playing over and over in my head like a song on repeat: What if they laugh at me? What if they laugh at me? What if they laugh at me?

I'M WAITING FOR THE BUS ON THE CORNER. MY

friend Jill comes up and stands next to me like she does every morning.

"What's up?" she asks.

"Nothin' much," I say, trying not to sound nervous about things.

"Really?" she says, not buying it for a second. "Why are you fidgeting with your fingers so much?"

I look down at my hands and I'm suddenly aware that I'm picking the ends of my fingernails. I do this when I'm nervous. Jill sees me everyday and knows that this is not normal.

"Oh, that," I say, trying to sound casual. "It's nothing really, just got a little case of the nerves."

"What are you nervous about?"

I start kicking my foot at a pile of dust that's formed by the side of the road. I stick my fingernails into my mouth and start chewing one off. "Just the dance recital tonight," I say through my hand.

"Oh yeah," she said remembering. She's not a dancer, but the recital is kind of a big deal. Everyone who's anyone goes to the Spring recital. It's kind of the official kick off to Spring - the time of year when the grown ups can officially celebrate the end of snow and the kids can get excited about not having to wear snow pants every time they want to play outside.

"Yeah, it's just that I'm pretty excited about it you know? We put a lot of work into all the dances and I just really want it to go well," I say, trying to downplay my nervous system's assault on my senses. I cram my fingernails back into my mouth and start rocking lightly from side to side.

Jill doesn't say another thing about it. She moves on, talking about how she has a crush on Chris Fredricks and how she thinks he's great and blah, blah, blah, blah. I stand there and listen to her because it's polite, but I couldn't care less about Chris or Jill's crush on him. The only thing that's on my mind is getting through the recital without messing it up.

Our bus driver, Mrs. Birdlo is almost always on time. But for some reason today, she's late. Coincidence? I think not.

SCHOOL FEELS WEIRD TODAY. I KNOW IT'S NOT, but to me it is. Everything seems to be moving slower than usual. Of course, I'm thinking about one thing and one thing only. And it is front and center making me a wreck. Before I left the house my mother told my to try not to think about it. Easy for her to say, she's going to be on the other side of the curtain. It's always easier to be the one watching the show, than it is to be the one in the show.

My father told me he couldn't wait to see it and that

he was sure it would be fine. He usually works pretty late and sometime he isn't even home for supper. I asked him if he was going to be there and he said, "I wouldn't miss it for the world, champ."

I know this should make me happy that my dad's coming and everything. I know not every kid has a dad that's as great as mine. But honestly, it totally adds an extra two layers of nerves. For one, I am now worried about whether he will make it or not. Because if he doesn't after he said he would, I will be crushed. And for two, if he does show up and I goof up in front of him, I will be crushed. You see what I mean, lose - lose. But then there's the third option. The one where he does show up and I don't flub my dance. And then he gives me hugs and tells me that he's proud of me. And that one's win - double win!!

I lost track of what my teacher said during math class and I'm trying to muddle through the practice problems. I've had to go up to her desk no fewer than five times. I've also had to ask my friend, Wendy, for help a few other times. Both of them are giving me strange looks. They have a right to I suppose. I am a straight A student and I never need help with my work. I'm usually able to pick things up very quickly.

At lunch I can barely eat what's in my lunch box. My mom always packs me awesome lunches, and today's no exception - except for the fact that I'm so nervous about that silly recital that it's all I can do to keep last night's dinner down, let alone worry about eating today's lunch.

"You okay?" My best friend Stephanie asks. "It's not like you not to eat."

"I know," I say, "but I'm just really nervous, that's all."

"About the recital? Don't be," she says so casually it nearly makes me sick. "You're a great dancer, you'll be fine."

A great dancer. Yeah, right. Who's she trying to fool? I would say I'm at best, a pretty good dancer. And that's on my best day of dancing ever, which I can already tell is not going to be tonight.

"Thanks," I say, unconvincingly.

She picks up on it right away, as only Steph can. If there's anyone in the whole world who was going to know when something's off with me, it's her. She and I have been friends since we were two. My mother and her mother are best friends and Steph and I spent a lot of time together when we were kids. I mean little kids.

"What do you want me to say?" I ask. "I mean, it's not like talking about it is really going to make it that much better, is it?"

"I don't know," she says, "why don't you give it a try?"

I think to myself for a moment. I think that what I've been doing hasn't really done anything to calm my nerves. It hasn't been helpful to keep it all bottled up and pretend that everything's alright. So, perhaps my bestie Steph is onto something.

"Okay," I begin. And then before I know it, the flood gates open and everything is out on the table. "And what if my dad doesn't show up? And what if my mom and dad are both there and I make a fool out of myself? And what if my brother laughs at me? And what if everyone else laughs at me? And what if I let everyone down and the Spring recital's ruined and it's all because of me?"

As I finish, she looks at me with the eyes of someone who wishes they could go back in time five minutes and take back their offer to listen. I can tell, now that I've told her everything, she doesn't really know what to say and there's no real way she's going to be able to help me.

"It'll be okay," she offers. But this really doesn't do much of anything.

I shrug my shoulders and zip up my lunch box. There's still ten minutes left in lunch, but I know I'm not going to eat anything. And then I just sit there staring off into space, imagining all that could go wrong. And Steph stares at me, probably thinking that she wishes she was friends with someone a little less crazy.

I think about how letting it all out and getting it out into the open was supposed to make things better. But it didn't. It made it worse. Far, far worse.

THE REST OF THE AFTERNOON WENT BY ABOUT the same as the morning. I couldn't get a hold of anything. Every lesson my teacher taught went right by me and all of the work seemed confusing and overly difficult.

Finally, it's time to get on the bus and go home. I get to try to take a few hours to relax before the recital.

As soon as I get through the front door, I head up to my bedroom and sit down on my bed. Then I lay down on my bed. Then I close my eyes. Then somehow, I manage to fall asleep.

I have a dream. It's the scariest dream I've ever had. And there aren't even any monsters in it or anything like that. I am standing in the wings - that's what we call the area just off the side of the stage. I'm waiting for my cue to run out and start my dance, but my cue doesn't come. I stand there for a second, not sure if I should go out or stay put. And then finally, I make the choice to go out onto the stage and give it my all. But when I try to move, I can't. My shoes have been glued to the floor. I panic and start to yell for someone to help me. And my yell is what ruins it. The other dancers look at me like I'm the worst person in the world because I've just ruined the show. The entire audience cranes their necks to get a look at the loud mouthed girl behind the curtain, the one who messed things up for everyone else.

I wake with a start and see my mom standing over me with my leotard and ballet shoes. I wipe the sweat from my forehead and declare that I'm not going.

"Don't be silly," she says.

"I'm not being silly," I tell her, as I stand up and walk across the room. "I just had the worst dream that I ruined the whole show for everyone."

She sits down and pats my bed and tells me to come sit next to her. "Honey, things are going to go just fine tonight."

"I know they are," I say, "because I'm not going. The recital will go off without a hitch."

"Sweet heart, listen to yourself. You are an important part of that recital, and to not go would be letting everyone down more than making a mistake in the middle of it."

"Yeah, right," I say.

"No really, Gina. You have people counting on you. They're counting on you to be there and they are counting on you to do the best you can in that moment. Now, if you want to sit up here in your room and let everyone else down, I'm not going to let you. Your friends and your dance instructor have worked too hard for one girl with a little case of the nerves spoil it for the entire dance group."

I don't even have a chance to respond before she shoves my outfit into my arms and says, "Put it on! We leave in ten minutes."

BACKSTAGE IS CHAOS. EVERYONE IS RUNNING around trying to get their costumes on just right, talking about their cues, and when they're supposed to go out on stage, and who they are supposed to stand next to, and when they do this move and that move. In some weird sort of way, this relaxes me. It's comforting to know you're not the only one.

My dance instructor, Miss Emily comes up behind me as I'm looking out onto the stage from behind the curtain. "You're going to be fine," she says. "Just loosen up, relax, and dance like you have for the last three months."

I look at her and smile in a way that tells her I need to hear more.

"You know what you're doing. The only difference is that tonight, you're doing it in front of people."

I nod my head spastically. I'm like a ballerina bobble head doll.

"Let me ask you a question," Miss Emily says. "Why dance?"

"What?" The question catches me off guard. I don't know what she's getting at.

"Why dance? If you can't share your expression with people, why do it?" She crouches down and brings her eyes down to mine. "This is why we do what we do. This is why we practice for months on end. This is why we deal with the pain. This is the reason. Right here. Tonight."

She stands up and walks away and suddenly I know what she means.

The show is about to begin and everyone is frantically running around trying to get set up for the beginning of the performance. I take one last peek out past the curtain and see my dad running down the aisle and taking his seat next to mom. I suddenly feel warm inside. I know that all I have to do is my best and that's going to be enough. At least for tonight. At least right now.

The music begins and the first set of dancers embark on the stage. I take my spot just behind the curtain, stage left, and with renewed confidence, I wait for my cue.

Sarah and the Search for the Pot of Gold

Justin Johnson

SARAH AND THE SEARCH FOR THE POT OF GOLD

THE BELL RANG AND SARAH PUT ON HER RUBBER boots and rain coat. Her feet squeaked loudly as she walked down the hall toward the doors.

"Sarah, wait up!" Sarah's best friend Amber was trying desperately to catch up, all the while trying to pull on her jacket and get her back pack zipped. This was typical of Amber, always a little rushed and disorganized.

Sarah turned to face her friend and almost got run over by an out of control sixth grader named Bernie Beeman. He was big and clumsy and apparently needed to change his brakes. He swerved, just narrowly missing her and grazing his shoulder against a set of lockers.

Sarah rolled her eyes and turned her attention back to Amber. "What's up?"

"Nothing, I just wanted someone to walk with."

"Okay." The two began walking toward freedom. It had been a tremendously boring day. Their teacher, Mr. Burns had stood up at the front of the room droning on and on and on and on. The worst part was that neither Sarah, nor Amber could even begin to remember what it was he had said.

"Did Mr. Burns say we had homework? Or not?" Amber asked, her backpack still only half zipped.

"I think he said to read."

"Wasn't there something else? I could've sworn there was something else." Amber finally threw her bag over her shoulders as she shrugged them. "Oh, well. I guess it couldn't have been too important."

The two reached the front doors and braced themselves for the rain to hit their faces. It had been raining buckets all day and Sarah was not looking forward to the walk home.

But then she noticed something. Something that changed her mind about the walk and something that changed her mind about going home.

THE SUN HAD COME OUT FROM BEHIND THE clouds and was now shining against the falling rain. This made Sarah excited. Amber, though she appeared to be nonchalant about the whole homework thing, was still thinking about it and didn't notice the full rainbow that had formed in the eastern sky.

"Do you see that?" Sarah asked, staring at the wonder in awe.

Amber said, "Hold on a minute, I'm thinking about something."

"You really should look at this," Sarah insisted. She nudged her friend hard on the arm, forcing Amber to look up.

"Wow, a rainbow," Amber replied, clearly disinterested. "Big deal."

"*Big Deal? Big Deal?* How can you say that Amber?" Sarah reached over and took Amber by both shoulders, giving her a firm shake. Their eyes met. "Do you know what a rainbow means?"

"Yeah, it means the sun was out when it rained."

"No, it means that somewhere out there, there's a pot of gold for the taking."

"What are you talking about? That's kids stuff Sarah. You can't be serious." Amber kept her eyes on Sarah, focusing on the corners of her mouth, hoping to spot a quiver or something that would let her know Sarah was joking.

"I am absolutely, without a doubt, one hundred percent serious."

"Okay, so you think there's a pot of gold at the end of the rainbow, what does that have to do with us?"

Sarah got a crazy look in her eyes and then she turned and started walking in the direction of the rainbow.

"Sarah," Amber called, "what're you doing? That's not how we get to your house. Your house is this way!"

Sarah kept walking and did not acknowledge Amber's pleas. Amber, after giving things the smallest moment of thought, decided that it was her job to go help her friend. She let out a giant sigh and took off running after Sarah.

"Sarah come on! Your mom's going to kill you. You know we have to go home right after school." Amber's attempts went unnoticed as Sarah continued on her path, heading straight for the end of the rainbow. It took her across the school parking lot and up the big hill to the playground and then through the woods surrounding the school. The whole time they were walking, Amber was right at Sarah's side chastising her for not listening.

Finally, when they had reached the end of a dead end street with nothing but forest facing them, Sarah looked up. She pointed, "Do you see that Amber?"

Amber looked up. "See what?"

"We are directly beneath the rainbow." She drew her gaze down and pointed into the mess of brush and trees. "And through those trees is where we'll find it."

"Why are you doing this, Sarah? Your mom's going to be worried sick about you, not to mention my parents will be worried sick about me too."

"I understand that Amber, I do. But what if you had

the chance to go after something so amazing, like the pot of gold, and you didn't because you were afraid to get into trouble?"

Amber mulled it over in her mind, giving it some serious thought. She looked up at the rainbow, which seemed so close now that she could just about reach up and touch it. She pulled back the sleeve of her rain jacket and checked the time. It was almost 4:30.

"Alright," she finally said, "we'll go look for the pot of gold. But if we haven't found it by the time it starts to get dark, we have to head home."

"Deal," Sarah said.

The two made their way through the brush and trees and soon were deep within the woods, searching for the pot of gold and ignoring their parents' wishes.

THEY WALKED A LITTLE WAYS WITHOUT SAYING A word. And then Sarah's thoughts turned toward all of the gold she'd find when they got to the end of the rainbow.

"So what would you do with the money?" She asked Amber.

"I don't know. I suppose I'd spend it on some new shoes or maybe some lip gloss. But it doesn't really matter anyway because we're not going to find it. It doesn't exist."

"Oh ye of little faith," Sarah poked. "Me, if I found the money, I'd buy the biggest mansion and hire a bunch of people to do my homework and go to school for me. I'd make sure that I had all the time in the world to do every-thing that I wanted to do. Nobody would ever bother me or make me do something I didn't want to."

"Mmm," Amber said thinking about this. After a minute she replied, "Nope, I think I'd still take the shoes and the lip gloss."

They'd been walking for a while. It was hard to see if it was really beginning to get dark, or if it was just the cover from the trees. Amber tried to check the time on her watch, but all the shade made it difficult, nearly impossible really, to see the green and black digital read out.

"We should probably start to head home now," Amber finally ventured. Her voice was shaky and it was clear to Sarah that she was quite nervous.

"Just a little longer," Sarah said, "Don't worry. We're almost there, I can feel it."

Against her better judgement, Amber continued to walk with her friend instead of turning around. She knew they should head home; knew that this was irresponsible and inconsiderate. But this was Sarah, and to be friends with Sarah meant you took the good with the bad. Unfor-tunately, when Sarah got going, her selfish streak was often enough to get both of them into a great deal of trouble. Amber guessed that Sarah thought finding the pot of gold would be enough for them to buy their way out of any trouble that might come their way.

Another hour passed and there was no question that it was dark, and not just the trees providing extra shade. They walked along unable to see anything. Amber was feeling frightened, wondering about the creatures that were in hiding behind the trees. They had to slow their pace to avoid tripping on stray twigs and branches.

Sarah, on the other hand, though she'd slowed her pace to allow Amber to keep up, was not frightened in the least. The rainbow had disappeared, setting with the sun. This didn't matter to her at all, however.

"Sarah, let's turn around," Amber begged. She was tired and hungry. What was worse, her mother was making her favorite, spaghetti and meatballs, for dinner. And she wouldn't even be there to have any - though, she didn't really think they'd be eating without her. She imagined them all sitting around the table, her mother and father and baby brother William, unable to eat because they were too worried about their only daughter. How stupid she'd been to follow her friend Sarah. She knew this was going to happen and yet she did exactly what she does every time: follow Sarah into trouble and trust her empty promises.

"We're not turning around. Not when we've come this far," Sarah said firmly.

"We can't even see the rainbow anymore. How do you even know where we're going? There's no way to be sure we're on the right track."

"Just be patient and keep walking forward," Sarah said, now picking up the pace and leaving her friend to struggle through the brush alone.

"Sarah, please slow down. We need to turn around and go home."

"Nonsense poopy pants," Sarah joked. Amber was clearly not amused. "Oh, why are you so uptight anyway?"

"I've already told you several reasons we shouldn't be here. Do you really need me to list more?"

Sarah thought about this for a second, partially because she'd paid no attention to Amber in the first place and partially because she knew it would aggravate her.

Just as Amber was getting ready to offer another reason why they should go home, Sarah noticed something.

"Do you see that?" she asked. It was glowing, a soft yellow coming from behind a thick tree. "There it is."

SARAH RAN TOWARD THE TREE. AMBER GAVE

chase trying to stop her friend from getting them into something else they wouldn't be able to get out of.

"You really should be careful Sarah. Don't just rush through there. You don't know who's back there. Maybe it's an escaped criminal hiding out?"

"Ah, where's your sense of adventure?" Sarah mocked, ignoring Amber yet again.

When they got up to the tree they slowed down. So many thoughts were going through Amber's head. They should go home, they shouldn't be here, she never should've let Sarah talk her into this, they shouldn't go around this tree, something really bad could be on the other side awaiting them... and what was that homework that Mr. Burns had assigned?

Sarah only had one thought going through her mind: *The pot of gold is on the other side of this tree!*

Doing her best to hide her giddiness, Sarah tiptoed around tree and to the other side. She stopped when she saw what was there. Amber bumped into her and fell down to the ground. When she picked herself up and dusted herself off, she couldn't believe what she was seeing.

For there, in the middle of a tiny clearing was a big black cauldron. It had to have been big enough for Amber and Sarah and two more people to climb in and hang out. But there was no room for that. For in this giant cauldron was all of the riches Sarah and Amber had ever hoped for.

Sarah smiled at Amber and for the first time on their journey, Amber smiled back. Sarah started licking her lips and rubbing her hands together like a greedy maniac.

"Come here, my beauty, my precious," she said and she stepped closer to the pot of gold.

"You might want to hold off on that and be a little more careful," Amber called. She stayed where she was, feet firmly planted as she watched her friend move swiftly in the direction of the gold. But it was pointless. Sarah was on a mission and it was clear that she could not and would not be stopped by anyone.

As she drew closer to the pot of gold, Sarah could feel the anticipation bubble up from deep within. Her feet and hands became cold, startlingly so. And her stomach, which just a few moments ago had absolutely nothing in it, now seemed to have butterflies fluttering around.

She stepped closer still and was almost to the point where she could put her hand out and actually touch the gold! Oh, the things she'd be able to do with it. No more homework, no more parents and teachers telling her what to do all the time. She'd be free! Free at last!

Or so she thought. For as she got closer, and it became time to grab for a piece of gold, a man jumped out from behind the cauldron and slapped her hand with a walking stick.

"Ow," Sarah cried, jumping back instinctively. She could hear Amber behind her crying and sniffling in the darkness.

In the glow of the gold pieces that illuminated the cauldron and the few feet surrounding, there stood a tiny man. He was smaller than Sarah and his clothes were green and tattered. There were patches in the knees of his pants and the elbows of his jackets. He had red hair and his face looked worn and weathered.

"What's the big idea!" He scolded.

"N..n..n.othing, s..s..sir, h..h..honestly," Sarah stammered. For the first time all day, she was unsure of herself, questioning what to do and wondering what she'd gotten herself into.

The little man walked, or rather hobbled, to the front of the cauldron, leaning heavily on his walking stick. Somehow, even coming up only to Sarah's chest, the little man was intimidating. Now that he was close, Sarah could see the cracks and wrinkles on his face. And she could smell the stench of him. He smelled as though he hadn't taken a bath in months, perhaps longer.

"Come on, Sarah," Amber urged, "It's time to go. We need to head home now."

"Oh, what's your rush?" The man asked. "You just got here."

"W..w..e have p..p..eople w..w..waiting f..f..for us at h..h..ome," Sarah stuttered.

"Ah," thought the man aloud. And then scratching his head he said, "So, let me get this right. See if I follow. You two, have come all the way into the woods in search of me pot of gold?"

Sarah nodded.

"And you arrived here at the gold quite late. It's been dark for the better part of an hour, in fact?"

Sarah nodded.

"And now that a wee scary little man has popped himself out from behind the pot that you though you were just gonna walk off with, you have to go home?"

Sarah nodded again, unable to find her voice.

"Well, let's get one thing clear," said the man, stepping closer, "that's my gold. And you're in my woods. And I've been following you for a very long while. And you know your friend there?" He tipped his head in Amber's direction. "She's been right the whole time. Not about my pot of gold, maybe, but about everything else. It's not very safe for girls like you to be out and about in the middle of the cold, dark night. Especially exploring woods and forests you've never been in before."

Sarah took a step back and was getting ready to run, when the little man grabbed her by the arm. Sarah turned and looked at him, fear in her eyes and heart.

"Before you go," the man said, not letting go of his grip, "you need to make me a promise."

Sarah nodded.

"You need to promise me, and all my buddies, that you and your friend there will never go on a search for a pot of gold as long as you both shall live. The gold's been spoken for, and it's not yours. And furthermore, you need to tell everyone of your friends and classmates that you've met a real live leprechaun." He brought his face close to Sarah's and when he spoke again, his voice was a whisper. "And we're not the nicest of creatures."

And then he let out a tremendous roar that startled both girls into running in the direction from which they came, both of them feeling like they'd never step foot inside these woods or any woods ever again.

NOW, I KNOW WHAT YOU'RE THINKING? WHAT happened to Sarah and Amber?

Well, let this be a lesson to you. The two did, thankfully, arrive home safely. However, they were very late and their families were very displeased with them.

Amber's mother forbade her to see Sarah any more. Of course, the two girls still saw each other at school, but they couldn't hang out after school or on weekends. And what's more, Amber didn't even speak to Sarah when they were in school. You see, after this experience, Amber went home and thought long and hard about what it means to be a friend. And she decided that a person like Sarah, who only does what she wants to do, no matter who it hurts, is not a person she feels comfortable calling a friend.

And what of Sarah? Well, she was grounded for a very long time. She, of course, was upset that Amber was no longer speaking to her, yet she didn't quite seem to understand why. People like Sarah never quite do. She has vowed to never go into the woods again in search of a pot of gold, or anything else. And to this day, Sarah is unable to drink green milk, enjoy a Shamrock Shake, or eat those tiny gold wrapped chocolate coins when St. Patrick's Day rolls around.

A KID IN KING WILLIAM'S COURT

JUSTIN JOHNSON

A KID IN KING WILLIAM'S COURT

JARED GREY LOVED BOOKS. HE LOVED THEM more than anything in the world. Yet, as he sat here on a cold September night, he found himself surprisingly displeased. It wasn't that the book was boring really, at least it hadn't been the first hundred times he'd read it. But that was the problem wasn't it?

The fact, that as he stared at his bookshelf, a monstrous thing - chock full of books, he couldn't help but feel a little dejected that he'd read every book on the shelf at least twenty times.

He was about half way through the book he was reading on this occasion, an old favorite about trolls and witches. But tonight it was not holding his interest. Flipping to the front cover, he looked at the picture and sighed. He tossed the book to the end of his bed and lay back.

Lacing his hands behind his head, he proceeded to stare at the ceiling. Eggshell white, with a few smudge spots from things he'd thrown a bit too high over the years.

He rolled over on his side. *I should go downstairs*, he thought to himself. But, he didn't want to. His mother was downstairs cooking dinner. And it wasn't that there was anything wrong with his mother, she was actually really awesome. He just wanted to be alone.

This was his time in the day to unwind, to lay low, to be free of responsibility. He'd finished his homework when he got home and then it was up to his room for freedom! The problem was, it was boring up here.

So, he had a choice to make: Stay up in his boring room and have a difficult time enjoying his freedom, or go downstairs and spend the whole time wishing he was upstairs in his boring room trying to enjoy his freedom. Ultimately, he decided to stay put.

At about 4:30, his father came home from work. Jared heard the kitchen door that attached the garage to the rest of the house slam shut. Followed by the hard and hollow sounds that his father's shoes made on the tiles of the kitchen floor.

"How was your day, dear?" he heard his mother ask.

"It was a fine day, honey. How about yours?"

"Nothing out of the ordinary, but it's good to be home."

And then Jared heard the words that made his ears perk up.

"Say," his father began, "Is Jared home yet? I have something for him?"

"He's right upstairs. You know how he is, always has his nose in a book," his mother laughed.

Jared then heard the sound of his father's footsteps coming up the stairs toward his room. The door opened and in walked his dad, dressed in a fancy suit. He still smelled of cologne, even after a hard day at work.

"Hey buddy, how was your day?" his dad asked.

"It was okay, how was yours?"

"Pretty good. I can't complain." His dad took a seat next to him on the bed and pulled his hand from behind his back. In his hand was a brand new book! A brand new hard cover book, with a nice shiny dust jacket and a picture of knight on a horse in front of a humongous castle. "I got you a little something."

Jared reached out and took the book from his father. "Aww, gee. Thanks dad! You're the best!" He leaned over and gave his father a tremendous hug.

After the embrace his father stood up. "Well, sport, I'll leave you to it. I have to go get changed into something a little more comfortable."

Jared sat on his bed rubbing his hand over the glossy

dust jacket as he watched his father leave the room. It was starting to get dark. He leaned over and turned on the lamp next to his bed. Removing the dust jacket and opening the book, Jared began to read.

THE STORY WAS AMAZING. IT GRIPPED JARED, just as the cover had. It was about a group of knights in a far off land. They lived in a wondrous castle and protected King William. The king was a fair and kind King. However, there was a king who lived in a nearby land who was not so fair and kind. He was called King Flagstaff and he wanted only to conquer King William's castle and all of his lands.

As Jared read on, he learned that the nice king was the father to a beautiful princess. Her name was Princess Kathryn. And she, like her father was fair and kind. Well, it turned out that King Flagstaff wanted to take Princess Kathryn to help him rule his kingdom.

Jared's mom popped in about an hour into his reading.

"Honey, it's time for dinner."

"Okay," Jared said. He found an old scrap of paper that had been on his night stand and put it into the book to save his spot. Staring at the book the whole way out of his room, Jared reluctantly put his head down and joined his parents for dinner.

He couldn't eat fast enough. All he wanted to do was get back to that book and that story and those characters. But the rule was you had to clean your plate.

"Slow down there, pal," his dad said, eyeing him strangely. "No one's going to take it from you now."

"I know," Jared managed through a bite of mashed potatoes.

"So honey," his mother asked, "do you like your new book?"

"Love it." This came out garbled as Jared once again struggled to speak through his food.

It took a while, but finally dinner was over and Jared could head back to his bedroom and settle back in with King William, Princess Kathryn and that evil King Flagstaff.

And boy, did he ever. It seemed like no time had passed before his father peeked his head in to check on Jared.

"I just wanted to make sure you're still alive in here," he joked.

"Very much so," Jared answered quickly, his eyes never leaving the book.

"Well, you'll want to think about putting the book up for the night, son. It's getting late and you have school in the morning."

"I will, dad," Jared yawned. "Only a few more pages, I promise."

"Okay, but don't say I didn't warn you."

And with that, Jared's father closed the door and left Jared to his reading.

THE STORY WAS JUST GETTING TO THE GOOD part and it was as if Jared was there. And then he smelled it. Grass and horses and sweat. He could hear the pounding of a thousand hooves and he could feel the ground shake beneath him.

He looked up just in time to see hundreds of horses charging at him, each one mounted by a knight in armor. Though the armor was not shining, it was actually quite scuffed up and had many a dent.

At first he didn't know what to do, but he eventually got his wits about him and took off running in the other direction. And then he noticed hundreds of horses coming from that direction, each with their own knight.

This was quite the bind he found himself in, and at the moment he had no way out. He looked around for the comforts of his room, his bed, his bookshelf, his night stand...even the door to the rest of the house. But all were gone.

Quick, he thought, *think of something, anything.* And then he looked down for his book. It was gone.

He looked back up and stared at the horses coming at him. And then he turned around and stared in the horses coming from this direction. He froze, not sure what to do.

"Get out of the way, lad," yelled one of the knights. Jared looked from side to side, unsure where the knight wanted him to go. "Oh for heaven's sake." The knight reached down a hand as his horse ran by Jared. He grabbed Jared by the back of the shirt and threw him onto the back of his horse.

Jared landed with a thud and quickly realized that riding a horse was a lot harder than it seemed.

"Who are you?" Jared asked.

"No time to discuss such things now," returned the knight. "We are in the middle of a battle."

"Battle for what?"

"The King of Flagstaff hath taken the beautiful and royal Princess Kathryn. The fair and honorable King William hath given us the charge of finding her and delivering her safely back to the kingdom."

Flagstaff?

Kathryn?

King William?

"Oh my God!" Jared heard himself saying instinctually.

"Dost thou use the name of the Lord in vain!"

"Sorry," Jared said.

The knight took a look over his left shoulder and then one over his right shoulder. As abruptly as Jared had arrived, the horse stopped and changed direction one hundred and eighty degrees. They were now riding past the a group of charging horses and into the woods.

When they were out of sight and protected by trees, the knight dismounted his horse. He grabbed Jared and helped him to the ground roughly.

"What are you?" The knight asked Jared.

"A...person?" Jared said, more a question than an answer.

"A person, you say." The knight brought his glove covered hand up to his chin and raised his eyebrow beneath this helmet. "An odd specimen of a person, for sure. But one that my prove useful."

"Useful?" Jared asked, a lump formed in his throat.

"Yes, useful," said the knight. "You see, the lovely Princess Kathryn is just on the other side of that field. She's been captured by King Flagstaff's lot and stowed away back in those woods."

"And that involves me how?"

"Well, my boy, it would probably be very simple for you to skirt around the battle in the middle and stick to the edge of the field." The knight gave Jared a look, like he was studying him for something. "And your size and stature would make it fairly easy for you to go unnoticed." The knight got a smile on his face as though he'd just thought of the best plan ever. He'd be the hero for sure for coming up with this one. "Absolutely, my boy - you are going to retrieve the fair princess for us this afternoon."

The knight mounted his horse and prepared to head back into battle. He pointed out toward Jared's left and said, "Head out in that direction. Move slowly at first and make sure they don't see you."

He gave his mighty horse two kicks with his feet and was off.

Jared stood in the middle of the thicket, suddenly wanting to be anywhere but here.

GREAT, JARED THOUGHT. *NOW WHAT HAVE I GOTTEN myself into.* Jared was an observer by nature, more willing to watch someone else take a risk, than to actually take one himself. Perhaps, that's why he enjoyed reading so much - because he was always watching someone else take the risk.

He moved through the trees in the direction of the edge of the field. It was hot and muggy and he could feel the black flies and mosquitos start to gather on his sweaty skin.

He moved close to the tree line and prepared to make

his move. From here he could see no less than two hundred men doing battle on horse back, bringing swords down and shields up. Although these men were adept at the art of battle, Jared couldn't help but think that it looked much more labored and clumsy than he though it would. This certainly wasn't a Netflix movie he was watching. It was dirty and smelly and just plain messy.

He crouched down and prepared to make his move. Though he liked to read, Jared also played on his school's soccer team and had earned the nickname "Grey - Hound" because he was as fast and agile as a greyhound dog. His long legs and smooth gate, the one that had helped him so many times before on the soccer field was now certainly needed here as he prepared to take off down the side of the battle field.

Jared removed a medal from beneath his shirt. It was dangling on a necklace that he wore everywhere he went. It had the imprint of a pair of shoes with wings. It had been given to him at the end of the soccer season. The team had a dinner at a local restaurant and awards had been given out. Jared had won fastest player, not just on his team, but for the entire league. He wore the medal like a badge of honor.

"Here goes nothing," he said to himself as he kissed the medal and slid it back into position beneath his shirt. He took two steps out of the woods and slowly began to work his way across the field.

The men on horseback didn't even notice him. Why would they, really? He was just a kid, small and scrawny compared to these men. He certainly wasn't capable of doing anything to them.

Once he noticed that nobody was paying any attention he increased his pace and before he knew it he was gliding across the field, his long loping legs making significant gains. Within a matter of a minute, maybe less, Jared had traversed the entire field and now found himself back in another insect filled woodland.

He had no idea where the princess was. And he couldn't really make any noise, as he was sure someone would've stayed behind to keep watch.

Bobbing and weaving from tree to tree, Jared made his way toward the back and center of these woods. He kept his eyes peeled for the sign of anyone who may be looking like a princess in distress. What he ended up seeing was something just a little different.

Princess Kathryn was perched against a tree, a rope around her legs and arms. She had dirt on her face and her hair was a mess. The red locks that Jared was sure would look so stunning, were instead greasy and thin. And the damsel in distress look that he was expecting her to have, was more the look of total boredom.

Jared looked around for some sign of a guard or warden, keeping a close eye on Princess Kathryn, but he found none. So, he moved a little bit closer. When he was no more than five feet away he called to her.

"Pssst. Are you Princess Kathryn?" Had he really just asked this? He could feel his face go flush with the instant embarrassment that such stupidity was known to cause.

The princess turned and looked at him. She couldn't have been any older than fifteen.

"That's me," she said sounding bored.

"Aren't you scared? You don't sound very nervous for someone who's tied to a tree with two hundred men fighting over you."

"I guess," she yawned.

"What's up with that?" Jared pressed.

"This happens all the time," she said. "I guess I've just kind of gotten used to it."

"How do you get used to this?"

"Well, really. I mean every day it's the same thing isn't it? Sure, sometimes it comes later, sometimes it's every couple of days - but really, it happens all the time."

"What happens all the time? This?"

"Yeah, this. I'm a princess in a book. Every time someone reads the book, this part happens. Sometimes the person who's reading the book comes to rescue me - thank you, by the way - but most of the time it's just Sir Doren. Here he comes now as a matter of fact."

Jared wasn't sure what to think. Sir Doren rode up to

them on his horse and dismounted. He extended his hand to Jared. "Sir Doren," he announced. "Thank you so very much for saving our dear, dear princess. Her father, the King will be so relieved to learn that we are getting her back."

"You're welcome," Jared said, although he felt like he hadn't really done anything.

"You will join us?" Sir Doren insisted.

"For what?" Jared caught a glance of the princess out of the corner of his eyes. She was nodding her head, bobbing it up and down emphatically.

"For the feast of victory," Sir Doren declared. "We've just won the battle thanks to you. It seems only fitting that you will be present to join us, doesn't it?"

Jared nodded. Sir Doren reached down and pulled Jared up onto the horse. He then nodded in the direction of the princess. "The usual, my lady."

"Yeah," she said. "I'm gonna walk home."

Jared watched as she took off through the woods, hopping and skipping and dodging tree roots and twigs. When she reached the clearing she gathered speed and took off on a sprint. Jared couldn't believe it. He thought she might even be faster him.

THE FEAST WAS EXTRAORDINARY. THERE WAS

music and food and drink and merriment had by all. When the feast was over the King stood up and everyone turned to listen.

"As you know," he began, "Our lovely princess, my lovely daughter, Kathryn was taken yet again this afternoon. I was very worried about her. For last time, some of you might remember, the child reading the book put it down so he could go and watch TV. Sadly, he has not returned to us."

Jared looked around, waiting for someone to pop out and say, 'gotcha.' But no one did. The King continued.

"More and more, Sir Doren has to rescue poor Kathryn and bring her back to us. It is becoming a sad state of affairs. However, today, we have much to celebrate and much to be thankful for. As young Jared Grey has managed to stick with it and finish the entire book - in one night no less. That is no easy feat, young man."

The King gave a tip of his head in Jared's direction and he was showered with applause and pats on the back.

"Furthermore, Jared is one of us now. He knows who we are and we know who he is. And it is with great pride and satisfaction that I extend this invitation to you, young Jared Grey. Don't be a stranger. And if you're sitting up in your room looking for something to occupy your time, please, don't hesitate to give us a visit."

Before he knew what had happened the King gave Jared a wink and a wave and Jared felt like he was falling.

His legs and arms were flailing and he braced himself for a crash landing that never came.

Rather, he startled himself awake. He moved his eyes back and forth and noticed that he was back in his room. The light of the early morning sun shone through his window, light bouncing off the book's dust jacket that had fallen onto the floor.

The bridge of his nose was sore and Jared noticed that the book was opened up flat against his face. He grabbed the book with both hands and lifted it up to read where he'd left off. He expected to be somewhere in the middle, but the page facing him now simply read 'The End.'

REVIEW

Dear reader,

I'm hoping if you enjoyed this story, that you'd be willing to leave a review for it wherever you bought it.

Reviews are very helpful in letting other readers know if they will enjoy a book, or not.

Thank you very much in advance for your time and effort.

Tootles,
Justin Johnson

YOU MIGHT ALSO ENJOY!

IF YOU ENJOYED THIS STORY, YOU MIGHT ALSO enjoy these!

WHEN JW FINDS OUT HE HAS super powers, he has to decide how he's going to use them. And he soon discovers, being a super hero isn't all it's cracked up to be! Click on the cover to read this exciting trilogy of superhero stories!

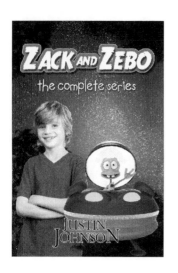

WHEN ZACK BENEFELD'S LIFE IS tipped upside down when an alien crash lands in his room, he has more than a few problems to deal with! Click on the book cover to read this fun story about a boy and his alien!

RICKY JENKINS WANTED A BUNNY for Easter. Mr. Whiskers was the runt of the litter. Now, Mr. Whiskers is over 200 feet tall and terrorizing the city! Click on the book cover to read this fast paced thrill ride!

WHEN EVAN TRIES TO TRAVEL TO PLUTO AND CRASH LANDS ON the North Pole, he gets the experience dreams are made of! Join

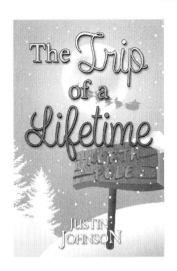

him as he learns all about he inner workings of Santa's Workshop! Click on the book cover to read this wonderful story that will get the whole family in the mood for the Christmas season!

Interesting Things Happen On The Island of Fru Fru

Gertrude loves to eat pizza and chug cola...and she's got a
bit of a weight problem.
But she's awesome at helping her friends defeat the
baddies who try to spoil all of the fun on the Island of
Fru Fru.
Click on the cover to reserve your copy today!

Should You Ever Go Back To The Past?

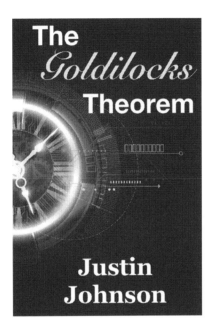

Jeremy wants to go back to the past to change the future.
But what he finds when he gets there is more than he
ever could have imagined.
Click on the Cover to Pre-order this Time Travel
Adventure!

What If You Were Put On the Naughty List?

One day, in the middle of a snowy Lincoln Street, Penelope Ann Dingman gets a letter that every kid dreads.

It seems she's been put on the naughty list.

But she doesn't know why.

With less than a week until Christmas, it's a race against the clock for her as she travels to the North Pole in hopes of having a private meeting with 'The Big Man' to set things straight.

Click on the book cover to pre-order this holiday tale!

You Might Also Enjoy!

I write...a lot! If you'd like to look through any of my books, feel free to click on the link above and check out my Amazon Author Page. Here, you'll find all of my books in all of their formats (ebook, paperback, and audio!).

Thank you for reading my stories!

Justin Johnson